To our loving parents and brothers for providing the inspiration to write the stories of Charlie Tractor™ and bring the fun adventures that we had to life for other children to enjoy.

www.mascotbooks.com

Charlie Tractor and Pickles

For more information, please contact:
Mascot Books
620 Herndon Parkway, Suite 320
Herndon, VA 20170
info@mascotbooks.com

Library of Congress Control Number: 2018901148

CPSIA Code: PRT0118A
ISBN-13: 978-1-68401-435-4

Printed in the United States

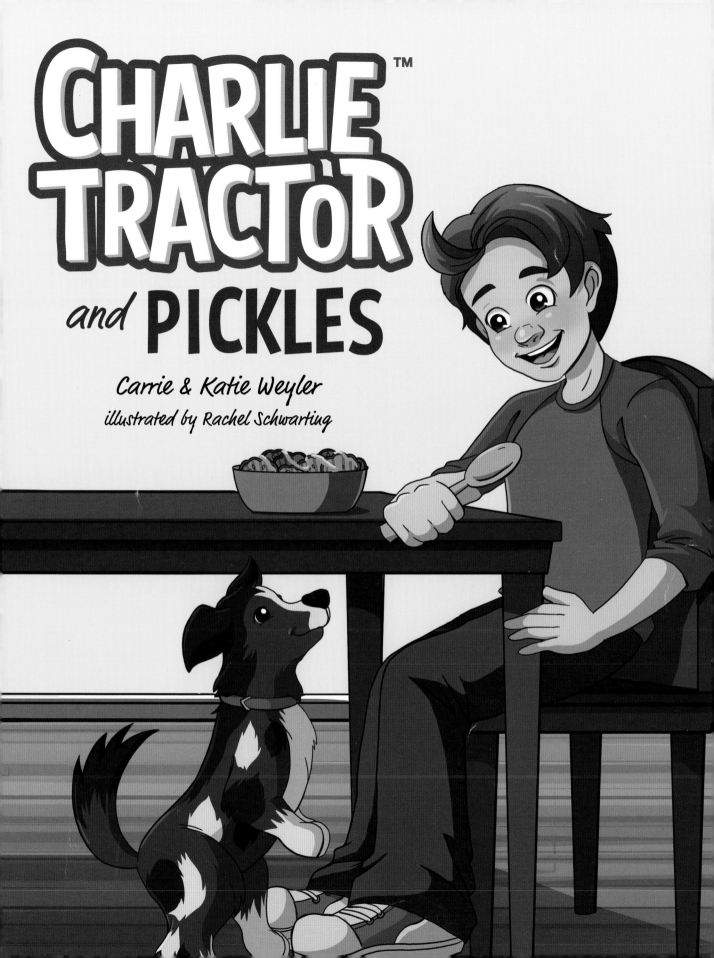

CHARLIE TRACTOR™
and PICKLES

Carrie & Katie Weyler

illustrated by Rachel Schwarting

Today was a special day for Charlie. He had been waiting all year for his dad to take him to pick out his very own dog. Charlie jumped out of bed excitedly and raced to wake up his mom and dad.

"Wake up! Wake up!" he shouted, running into their room.

"Just a minute, Charlie," his dad said sleepily. "Let's have breakfast first and then we'll go pick out your dog."

As Charlie and his dad arrived at the animal shelter, Charlie shouted "We're here! We're here!" They were the first ones to arrive at the shelter when it opened that morning.

There were lots of dogs and puppies at the shelter. Most of them were barking, so it was very loud!

Charlie's dad said, "Do you like this one?" pointing to a little white and tan dog in the second cage.

Charlie replied, "No, that dog is too small."

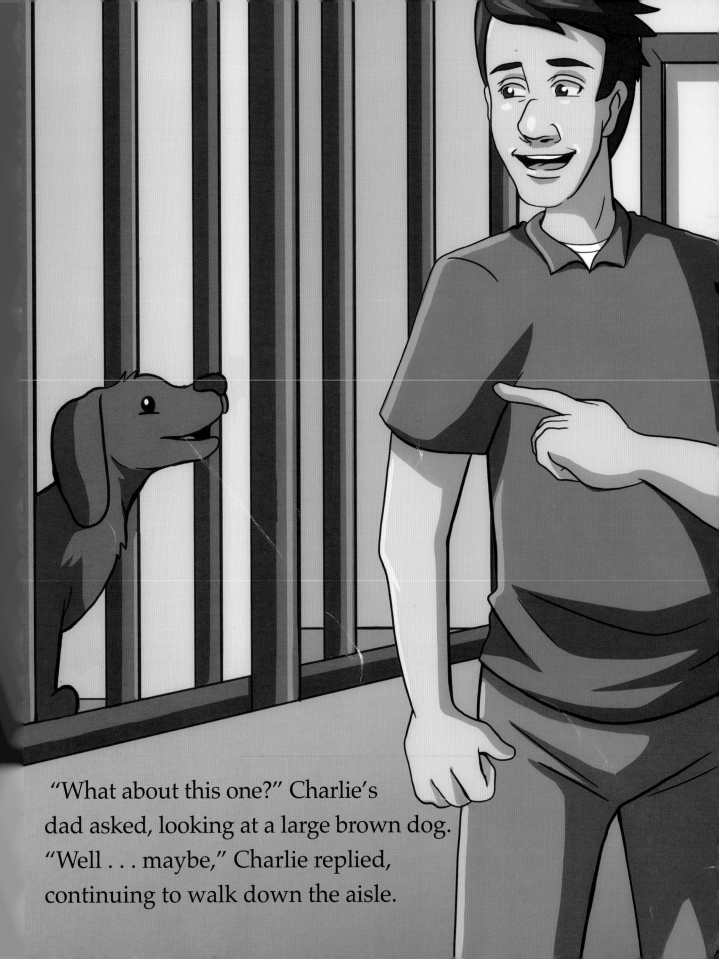

"What about this one?" Charlie's dad asked, looking at a large brown dog. "Well . . . maybe," Charlie replied, continuing to walk down the aisle.

Then all of a sudden, Charlie stopped and shouted, "This is the dog I want! This is him!" He was a medium-sized dog with black, brown, and white spots.

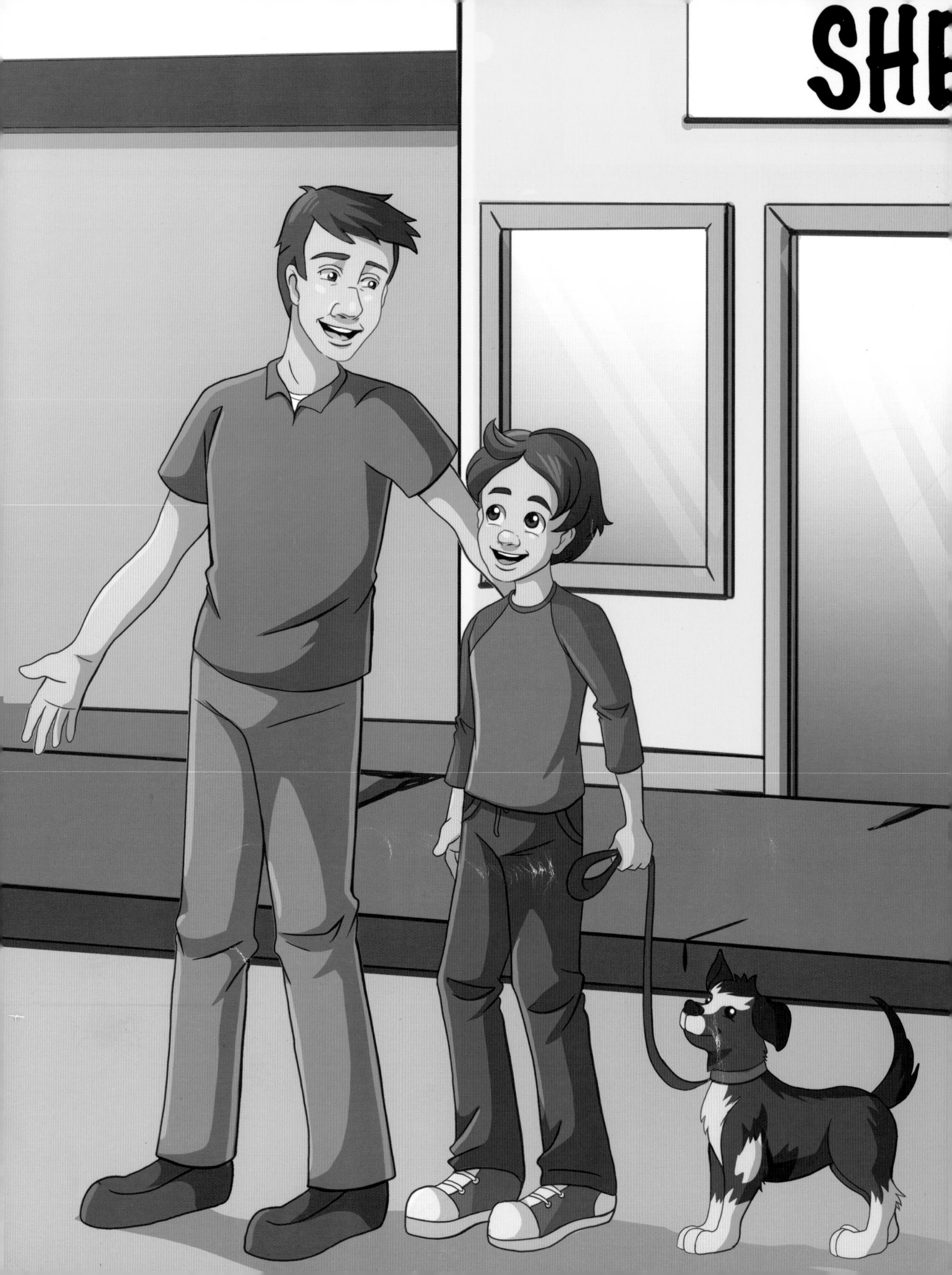
SHE

"Why did you pick this dog?" Charlie's dad asked. Charlie answered, "This one smiled at me when all of the others just barked!"

"Okay" Charlie's dad agreed happily. "I think he will be the perfect addition to our family."

Charlie's mom and sister, Tammy, were waiting eagerly by the front door to meet the newest member of the family when they got home.

Tammy wondered what Charlie was going to name his dog.

"What about calling him 'Spot'?"
Charlie's dad asked.
"Hmmm… maybe," said Charlie.

Charlie and Tammy thought and thought, trying to pick the perfect name for their new dog, when Charlie's dad asked, "Does anyone want me to make some mustard pickles for lunch?"

"Yeah!" Charlie shouted, "I love mustard pickles!" They were always one of Charlie's favorite snacks.

Charlie looked at his new friend with a grin and said, "Do you like pickles, too?" The spotted dog wagged his tail with a smile.

As Charlie sat down at the kitchen table, happily eating his mustard pickles, he noticed the dog jumping up and down, trying to sneak a bite.

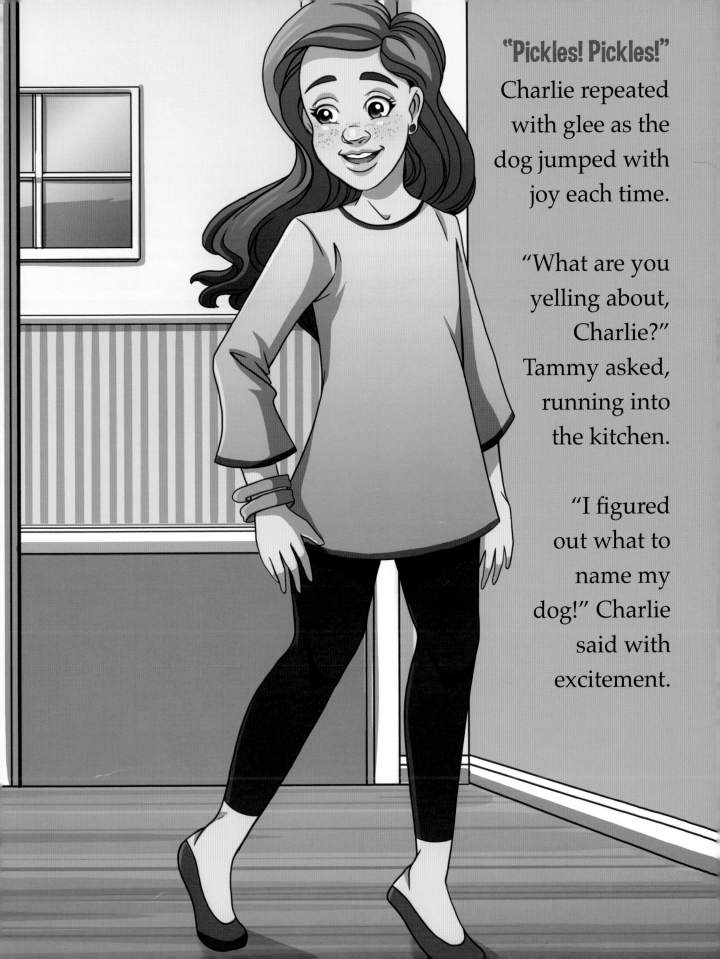

"Pickles! Pickles!" Charlie repeated with glee as the dog jumped with joy each time.

"What are you yelling about, Charlie?" Tammy asked, running into the kitchen.

"I figured out what to name my dog!" Charlie said with excitement.

"Everyone, meet... Pickles!"

"Pickles? That's a silly name for a dog!" laughed Tammy. "That's like naming a dog 'Broccoli'!"

"No it's not!" shouted Charlie. "I LOVE pickles, but I don't love broccoli!"

"Okay, Charlie," their dad replied, "We'll call him 'Pickles.' I think it's perfect."

Charlie and Pickles played games like hide-and-seek and fetch together for hours.

It was a great day!

That night at bedtime, Pickles laid beside
Charlie's bed. They both were very tired.

Charlie's parents whispered, "Good night" to Charlie and Pickles. Charlie replied, "Good night Mom and Dad. See you tomorrow."

THE END

ABOUT THE AUTHORS

Sisters Katie and Carrie Weyler grew up in Ohio. Katie is the oldest of five children, while Carrie is the youngest. They had a fun and adventurous upbringing, which inspired the stories of Charlie Tractor™.

Now, with families of their own, they have set out to retell the stories they imagined and experienced as children. These stories, based on actual events, share the adventures of Charlie Tractor™ and his family.

They hope that these stories bring enjoyment and laughter to you and your family as much as they did to Katie and Carrie.

ABOUT THE CHARLIE TRACTOR™ BOOK SERIES

These short, fun, colorful books were created for busy parents, grandparents, teachers, and others with children two to ten years old. The adventures of Charlie Tractor™ are happy, simple, family-oriented stories designed to hold the child's attention, teach a fun fact or two, bring laughter and enjoyment, and be read in less than ten minutes.

Connect with us at:
www.charlietractor.com
charlietractorbooks@gmail.com
Follow us on Facebook and Instagram

Have a book idea?

Contact us at:

info@mascotbooks.com | www.mascotbooks.com